Chester Bear, Where Are You?

written by
Peter Eyvindson
and illustrated by
Wendy Wolsak-Frith

PEMMICAN PUBLICATIONS INC.

Pemmican Publications Inc. gratefully acknowledges the assistance accorded to its publishing program by the Manitoba Arts Council, the Canada Council for the Arts and the Book Publishing Industry Development Program.

Printed and Bound in Canada
1st Printing 1988 • 2nd Printing 1993 • 3rd Printing 1993
4th Printing 1995 • 5th Printing 1999 • 6th Printing 2006
7th Printing 2010 • 8th Printing 2013

Canadian Cataloguing in Publication Data

Eyvindson, Peter

Chester Bear, Where are you?

ISBN 978-0-921827-08-5

1. Wolsak-Firth, Wend. II.Title.

PS8559.Y95C5 1988   jC813/.54   C88-098187-3
PZ7 .E98Ch 1988

PEMMICAN PUBLICATIONS INC.
Committed to the promotion of Metis culture and heritage
90 Sutherland Avenue
Winnipeg, MB R2W 3C7 Canada
www. pemmicanpublications.ca

for Linda

Konrad thought
it was funny the
night Kyle lost
Chester Bear.

And so did
Kristoffer.

But Kyle definitely
knew it wasn't funny.

Kyle knew big brothers didn't know any-
thing. They said that Chester Bear was just
a good-for-nothing, stupid old stuffed bear.
But Kyle knew better.

Kyle knew Chester Bear was his very best
friend.

After all, hadn't Chester Bear gone to
school that very first day?

Just to make certain that Kyle didn't get
lonely?

And didn't good old Chester Bear go just about everywhere with Kyle?

Chester Bear played with him in the sandbox.

He sat beside him at lunch time.

And when Mom sat down to read Kyle a story, Chester Bear would always snuggle up on Kyle's lap.

It was at night, though, when
Kyle had to go to bed, that
Chester Bear was really Kyle's
very best friend.

Because while Kyle slept, it
was Chester Bear who made
certain that snakes didn't
crawl out from under the bed.

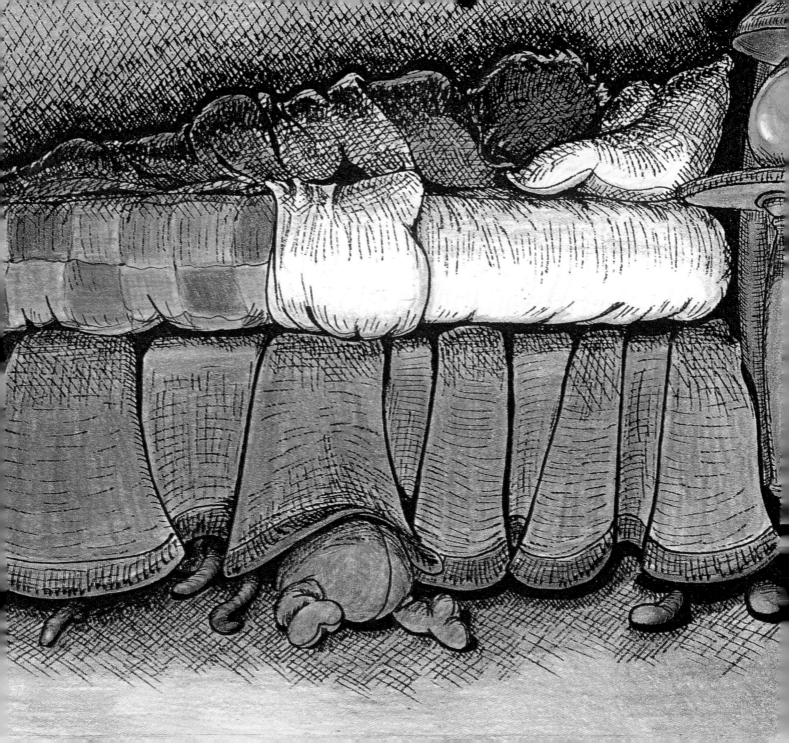

Or when those bad booglely men tried to sneak out of the bedroom closet, Chester Bear was always there to scare them away.

And that's why whenever he knew it was time to go to bed, Kyle would find Chester Bear.

But that night when Kyle
looked under the bed,
Chester Bear wasn't there.

He looked in the closet.
But Chester Bear wasn't
there, either.

He looked in the clothes
hamper, the waste basket,
the toy box, under the kitchen
table and behind the sofa.

But still, Kyle could not find
Chester Bear.

"Have you seen
Chester Bear?"
Kyle asked Konrad.

But Konrad just
laughed.

"Kristo," Kyle asked, "Have you seen Chester Bear?"

Kristoffer only murmured 'No,' because he was too busy playing a computer game.

"Dad," Kyle asked, "Have you seen Chester Bear?"

"What's that, son?" Dad couldn't help. He was too busy reading the newspaper to worry about Chester Bear.

"Never mind," Kyle said, "I'll get Mom to help. Mom always knows about Chester Bear."

But this time, Mom didn't know what had happened to Chester Bear.

"Did you look under the bed?" she asked. "How about your toy box? Behind the sofa?"

Sadly Kyle had to answer, 'Yes' each time Mom asked a question.

"Well then. We'll just have to look for him," Mom said. "He has to be somewhere."

Together, they looked everywhere for Chester Bear.

Upstairs. Downstairs. And in every room in the house. They still couldn't find Chester Bear.

Just to be sure, Mom looked inside the dryer and Kyle looked behind the toilet.

But still no Chester Bear.

"Maybe he's outside," said Mom. "Maybe you left Chester Bear out there in the sand box when you went out to play."

Mom got down a flashlight and together, they went outside.

But Chester Bear wasn't in the sandbox, either.

"What about the car?" asked Mom. "Did you leave him in the car when I picked you up after school?"

But Chester Bear wasn't out in the car. Mom even looked in the trunk.

Chester Bear couldn't be found.

Anywhere.

"Kyle. I don't know what we can do," Mom said sadly.

"I can't find Chester Bear tonight.   Maybe he'll turn up in the morning. It's getting late and you need to get some sleep."

Kyle knew he couldn't go to sleep.
Not without Chester Bear.

Chester Bear protected him from
the snakes under the bed and the
booglely men in the closet.

Without Chester Bear around,
they'd get him for sure.

"Get into bed, Kyle." Mom smiled as she gave him a hug. "Snuggle up with Toby for tonight. And tomorrow we'll look for Chester Bear."

"Toby," thought Kyle as he took off his bathrobe.

"What good is Toby? He's just a stupid old good-for-nothing stuffed bear.
Not at all like Chester Bear."

Sadly, Kyle climbed into bed and put his head on the pillow.

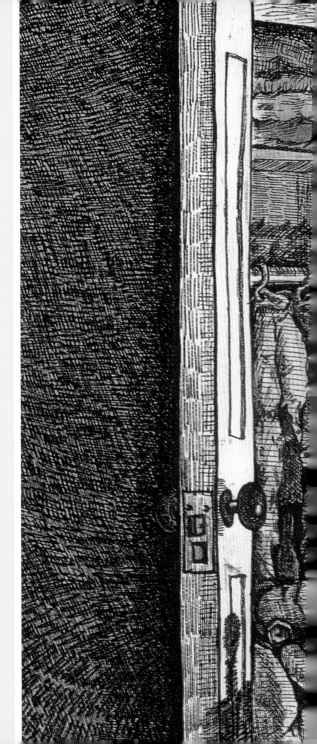

Wait a minute! Was that a hard lump under his pillow?

Was it Chester Bear?

It Was!

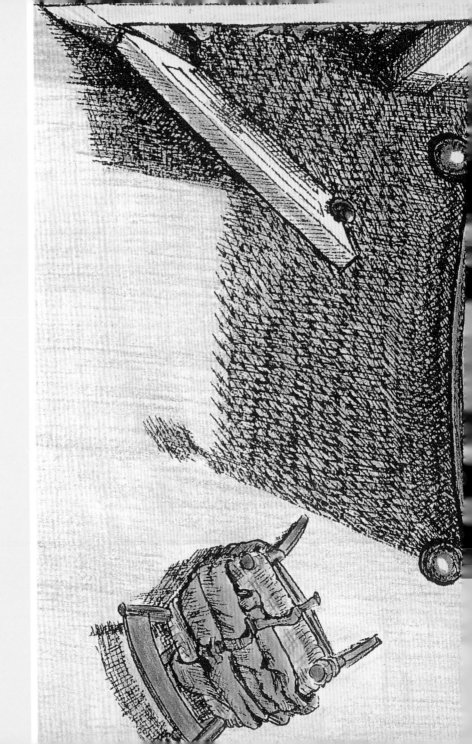

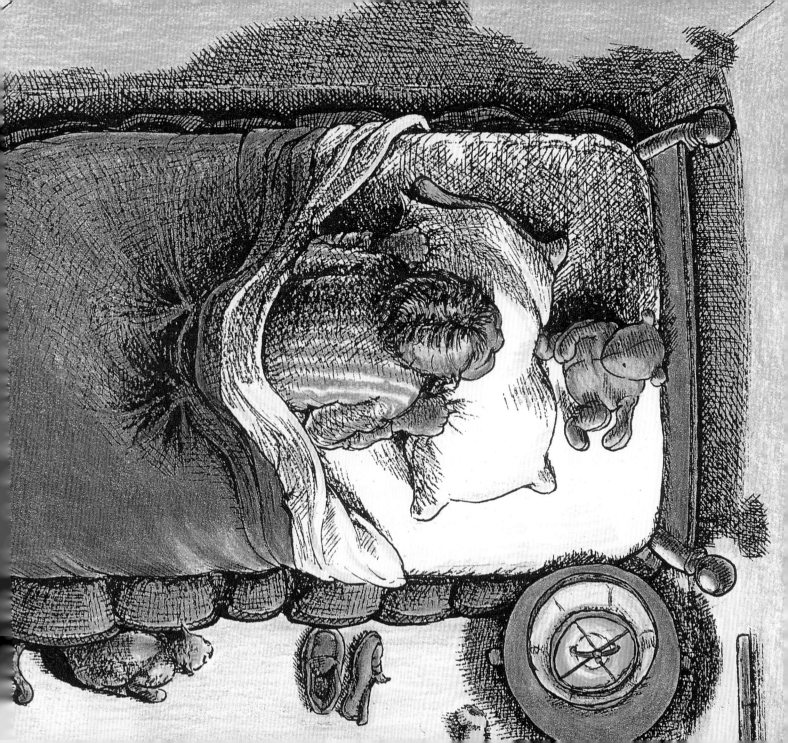

All the time, Chester Bear had been hiding under the pillow.

Chester Bear winked one glass eye and whispered a peek-a-boo that only Kyle could hear.

"Peek-a-boo yourself, you silly old Chester Bear," laughed Kyle as together they snuggled down under the covers and drifted happily off to sleep.

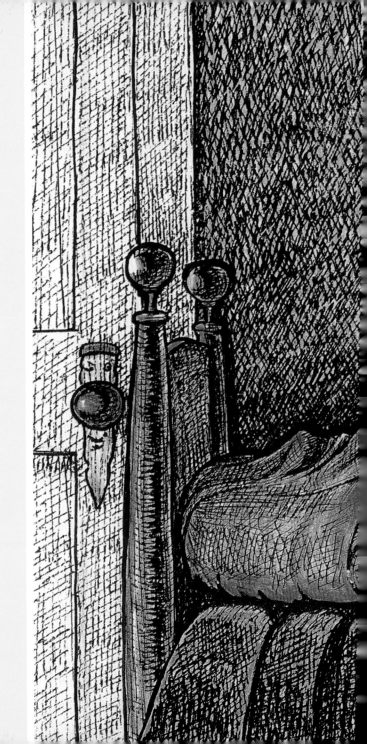